BENNY, BENNY BASEBALL NUT

by David A

illustrated by Kelly Oechsli

SCHOLASTIC INC.

New York   Toronto   London   Auckland   Sydney

ISBN 0-590-40379-6

Text © Copyright 1987 by David A. Adler
Illustrations © Copyright 1987 by Kelly Oeschli
All rights reserved. Published by Scholastic Inc.
LUCKY STAR is a trademark of Scholastic Inc.
Art direction by Diana Hrisinko
Book design by Theresa Fitzgerald

12 11 10 9 8 7   8 9/9 0 1 2 3/0

Printed in the U.S.A.
First Scholastic printing, March 1987   40

To Michael, Michael, Baseball Nut

"He's going back, back, back. He makes the catch."

That's my brother Benny. In the winter he's almost normal. But starting in March he begins to talk about baseball. And that's all he talks about.

"Here's the long throw to first. He's out."

Right now Benny is in the upstairs hall talking about a game between the Tonix and the Cashews. Those are teams in his Benny, Benny League. There are really no Tonix and no Cashew teams and there is no Benny, Benny League. Benny just pretends there are. Like I said, in winter he's almost normal. But this is the summer.

"We're in the ninth inning now. The score is tied, three to three."

I sat on my bed and tried to read. I was reading about blue whales. They're the biggest animals in the world. I'm real interested in anything that lives underwater.

"It's a hit. Johnson is trying for two. He's out!"

I closed my door. But I still heard him. So I stopped reading and listened. The game was getting exciting. "Simson is up. He swings and hits a soft grounder to first. Two outs."

Then Mom called us to dinner.

"Not right now," Benny told her. "The game is almost over."

I opened my door and walked toward the stairs.

"There's a break in the action," Benny said. "A girl has walked onto the field."

When I got to the stairs, Benny said, "And now, with two outs and the score tied, the Tonix second baseman, Benny Baker, steps up to the plate."

I knew what would happen.

"Benny swings. It's a long fly ball. It's out of here. It's another home run for Benny

7

Baker. That Baker is great!"

I knew it.

"Come on, Jane, let's go to supper," Benny said as he walked past me. He was smiling. "I just hit another home run."

I didn't talk much at dinner. I listened. It was funny listening to Mom, Dad, and Benny talk. Mom is a lawyer. She told Dad something about her first case. Benny thought she said "first base."

"You have to be tall to play first base," Benny said. "And you have to be able to stretch."

Dad said he had some *trouble* with his car. Benny thought he said *double*.

"I hit a double in our last game. It went right over third base."

When Dad said *couch*, Benny heard *coach*. When Mom said *patch*, Benny heard *catch*. Finally Mom said, "Is baseball the only thing you think about?"

I nodded. Dad smiled. But Benny, of course, didn't hear exactly what Mom said. He thought she asked him if he wanted to talk about baseball.

"Sure," Benny said. "We have a game tomorrow. The coach said if I practice my throwing, I can play third base."

"Practice with Jane," Dad said.

"But she's on another team."

We *are* on different teams. Benny plays for the Birds. I play for the Gum Drops. But we're in the same league. And the game tomorrow is between Benny's team and mine.

I'm a year younger than Benny and a year behind him in school. He was already playing on the Birds when I became old enough for the league. The local pet shop bought the uniforms, bats, and things for the Birds. And Mr. Tweet, the pet shop owner, brings a few

birds in cages to each game to cheer for the team. One of the birds talks, but all it says is "Hello" and "Crackers."

I joined the Gum Drops because all of my friends are on the team. A candy store sponsors our team. All during the game Mr. Cotton, the candy store owner, gives us gum drops, chewing gum, and chocolate. He says the candy gives us the energy to win. Dad says the candy gives us cavities. Dad is a dentist.

After dinner Benny and I practiced baseball in front of our house. He talked more than he caught.

I threw the ball to Benny.

"It's a ground ball to second baseman Baker," he announced. "He picks it up and makes the long throw." Benny threw the ball to me and I caught it. "One out," Benny said.

I threw the ball high into the air. Benny had to run back to catch it.

"It's a high fly ball," Benny said as he ran after it. Benny ran to the edge of the sidewalk. He reached out into the street and caught the ball.

"What a catch! What a catch!" Benny said. "Baker reached into the stands for that one. That Baker is great!"

Mr. and Mrs. Vine, two of our neighbors, were walking by with their dog. They clapped — the Vines did, not the dog. And they stayed to watch.

I threw ground balls, fly balls, and line drives to Benny. He caught some of them. He dropped some. And he announced them all. He sounded just like the baseball announcers we hear on radio and television.

"What's the score?" Mr. Vine asked.

"Seven to five. The Cashews are winning."

"Cashews?" Mrs. Vine said. "A cashew is a nut."

"So is Benny," I told her. "A baseball nut."

Chapter 3

When it got dark we went inside to watch television. I wanted to watch a special program about sea horses. They have long noses and big eyes and look like little horses. But they really are fish.

Benny wanted to watch a baseball game.

I turned on the television and set it for my program. "Sea horses are small," the announcer said in a real deep voice.

Click.

Benny changed the channel.

"It's the third inning. Big Belly Stevens is at bat. He sets himself and waits. Here's the pitch."

Click.

"A sea horse uses its long tail to wrap around things that grow underwater."

Click.

"That's a double for Big Belly Stevens. He stands on second base. Stinky Weber is the batter. Stinky takes a few practice swings. He. . . ."

Click.

"Sea horses are not strong swimmers."

Click.

"Stop it," I said. "How can I watch a program if you keep changing channels?"

My mother looked into the den and asked, "What's the problem here?"

"Benny wants to watch people named Big Belly and Stinky play baseball and I want to learn about sea horses."

"We're sharing," Benny said. "I let Jane watch her fish program for one minute. Then I switch to watch baseball for one minute."

"As long as you share," Mom said and she left the room. I did, too. I had seen enough baseball for one night.

I went to my room. I got ready for bed. Then I took out my book about blue whales and began to read it.

People hunt and kill blue whales for their oil. In some countries people even eat whale steaks. But now there are only a few hundred blue whales left in the world. If people keep killing them, soon they may be all gone.

"He swings and hits the ball way over the second baseman's head. But wait! Benny Baker jumps. He stretches. He catches the ball. Oh, that Baker is great."

I sat up in bed and saw Benny walk past. He was announcing another pretend game in his Benny, Benny League. I knew I couldn't read anymore. First I closed my book. Then I closed my light and my eyes. I tried to fall asleep.

"It's the end of the seventh inning," Benny announced. Then he went into the bathroom to brush his teeth.

"Glub, blubby, slurp, slurp."

Even while he brushed his teeth, Benny was announcing his pretend game.

My room is next to Benny's. There's just a thin wall between us. I heard Benny turn off his light and get into bed. And I heard him say, "The Tonix have runners on first and second. The score is tied, one to one."

I tried to imagine being on a boat with a glass bottom and watching fish swim by. That's my favorite dream. But Benny was talking too loud for me to dream about fish.

"Will Barrow steps up to the plate. He watches the first pitch whizz past. Strike one."

Then it started.

"The second pitch is a frog. He waves at the glue. It's a chicken soup."

It happens every night. Benny was falling asleep. He was no longer announcing a baseball game. He was announcing nonsense.

"Glob in the air. Ugh marble doughnuts. Chocolate chip. Glib, blip, gray."

Then he was quiet. Benny had fallen asleep. In a few minutes so did I.

The next morning Benny and I wore our baseball uniforms to breakfast. I had toast, orange juice, and pineapple cottage cheese.

Benny told Mom he wanted to eat steak, potatoes, and coffee.

"Coffee," Mom said. "That's not for children. And steak and potatoes are not for breakfast."

"But that's what Big Belly Stevens eats before a game."

"Big Smelly Stevens doesn't live in this house," Mom said. "You can have what Jane is having. You can have cereal. Or you can have eggs."

I laughed. Mom had called Benny's favorite player Big *Smelly*.

Benny took the box of Sweet and Sticky Corn Bips from the pantry and poured some into a bowl. "Big Belly doesn't eat Bips," Benny mumbled as he poured milk over the cereal.

"Today will be sunny," Mom said as she read from the newspaper. "It's a good day for a baseball game."

Benny said something but Mom and I couldn't understand him. He was having trouble with the Bips. They stuck to his teeth.

Mom and Dad drove us to the baseball field. The field was crowded when we got there. Some of the players on Benny's team, the Birds, were doing jumping exercises. A few of the others were having a catch. Benny got out of the car and ran to the ones having a catch.

My team, the Gum Drops, had all gathered

around Mr. Cotton. He's the owner of the candy store that sponsors our team. He was giving out little chocolate eggs, the kind with cream inside.

"Don't you take any of that candy," Dad told me. "You're here to play baseball, not to get cavities."

"What's the use of having a father who's a dentist if I can't get some cavities?" I said as I got out of the car.

Since I couldn't eat the candy, I watched Benny and his friends. The coach threw a ball to Benny. He caught it and threw it back. Then the coach threw the ball high into the air. Benny ran back and caught it.

Benny was doing great. He caught every ball that came near him. Then, as Benny reached up to catch a ball, I realized something was missing. Benny wasn't talking. I didn't think Benny could play baseball without announcing every play.

I looked more closely. The coach threw the ball high into the air. Another boy ran for it. I watched Benny. As the boy caught the ball, Benny's lips moved.

I was right. Benny couldn't play baseball without talking. He was too embarrassed to let his friends hear him, so he was talking to himself.

The seats along the side of the field were almost all taken. My parents were sitting behind first base. Mom was looking at some papers. Dad was talking to the old man sitting next to him.

Honk. Honk.

A small red truck was driven onto the field. *Honk. Honk.*

The door opened and Mr. Tweet jumped out. He's the owner of the pet store that sponsors the Birds. That's Benny's team.

Mr. Tweet stretched his arms out and said, "Here I am."

Mr. Tweet ran to the back of his truck. He opened the doors and took out two large bird cages. There was a bird in each cage.

"Hello. Hello. Crackers. Crackers," the bird in one of the cages said.

"I'm here," Mr. Tweet called out. "Let's get the game started."

Chapter 5

A man wearing a dark shirt and dark pants walked onto the field. He was the umpire.

"Whose truck is this?" he asked.

"It's mine," Mr. Tweet said.

"Well, get it off the field. We have a game to play."

The umpire called the coaches together. They talked for a while. The umpire blew a whistle. I ran to my team's bench. It was near third base.

"Our team gets to bat first," our coach told us. Then he read our batting order and told each of us where we would play in the field. I would bat fifth and be the right fielder.

I sat on our bench to watch. Benny was in the field in the second baseman's position. He was moving around a lot, punching his glove and calling out, "Let's go. Let's go. We'll beat these Gum Drops. We'll chew them up."

I wanted to call to him, "You'll get cavities if you chew gum drops." But I didn't.

"Play ball," the umpire called out.

Mr. Cotton gave Bobby Taylor, our first batter, a Yum Yum chocolate bar and said, "Hit a home run."

Bobby stood near home plate. He bit into the chocolate bar. The pitcher and catcher waited as Bobby ate the candy.

"Play ball," the umpire called again.

Bobby quickly pushed the rest of the candy into his mouth. He stood at the plate, held his bat up, and waited.

The first pitch was a strike. Bobby watched it go by. I think he was too busy eating his

Yum Yum bar to worry about hitting the ball.

Bobby stood there and didn't swing his bat once. He struck out. Then he walked back to Mr. Cotton and said, "That chocolate was great. Can I have another one?"

"Sure," Mr. Cotton said. He gave Bobby another Yum Yum. And he gave him some banana taffy.

Our next two batters got hits. The fourth batter, the one before me, struck out. Then it was my turn to hit.

Mr. Cotton gave me a Yum Yum bar and said, "This will give you energy."

"My dad says it will give me cavities," I said.

"Cavities," Mr. Cotton said. He looked at the Yum Yum and said, "I guess your dad is right." Mr. Cotton reached into his pocket. He took out a bag of roasted sunflower seeds and gave it to me.

I stepped up to home plate. I held up my bat and waited.

The ball seemed to just float in to me. I swung and hit the ball. But I didn't hit it well. The ball rolled slowly toward Benny. I ran as fast as I could.

"Hello. Hello. Crackers. Crackers," one of the birds called as I ran past.

I reached first base before Benny could get to the ball. I had a hit. A run had scored. We were winning.

"What a cheap hit," Benny said.

"It was a hit and that's all that matters," I told him.

I stood a few feet off first base. While I waited for the next batter I ate some sunflower seeds.

"Hello. Hello. Crackers. Crackers," the bird called to me. It started flapping its wings and going wild. Everyone was watching the bird and wondering why it was so excited. But I knew why. The bird saw the seeds I was eating and wanted some.

The umpire held up his hands to stop the game. I heard Benny whisper, "There's a break in the action."

The umpire walked to the bird cage and said, "Either someone quiets this bird or he'll have to leave."

I put my bag of sunflower seeds away. I didn't want the bird to have to wait in the truck.

Then the umpire told Mr. Cotton to stop giving candy to the team. "They're here to play baseball," he said, "not to eat."

The umpire ran behind home plate and called, "Play ball."

I had to watch what was happening. If the ball was hit, I had to run. As I watched, I heard something. It sounded like an announcer at a baseball game. It was Benny.

"Here's the pitch. Ball one.

"There are runners at first and third base. Here's the next pitch. The batter swings and misses. Strike one."

I wondered if anyone else heard Benny.

"Here's the next pitch. The ball is hit high into the air."

I ran. The ball was hit high over the pitcher's head. It was coming down right near second base, right to where Benny was standing. As I ran past, I heard him say, "Baker is trying for it. He jumps. He stretches. He has it for the third out. That Baker is great!"

Chapter 6

Benny didn't jump and he didn't stretch. But he did catch the ball. Our half of the inning was over. It was the Birds' turn to bat.

The Birds are a noisy team.

"Get a hit. Get a hit," one of their players kept calling.

"Let's go!"

"We have to win."

"Hello. Hello. Crackers. Crackers."

I was playing in right field, which is behind

first base. During the first inning, the ball wasn't hit to me.

The Birds made a lot of noise. But they didn't hit the ball very well. The first two batters hit easy pop flies, which were caught. The next batter swung and missed the ball three times for the third out.

During the rest of the game, Benny kept talking. A few times he talked loud enough for me to hear him. And I was sitting on the bench. Once during the game the Birds' pitcher turned around and said, "Turn off that radio."

"It's not a radio. It's Benny."

"Well, then turn off Benny."

There were no more runs until the last inning. During our half of the inning, Dabney Bell hit the ball on the ground. He didn't hit it hard but the Birds' third baseman let it roll under his glove.

Dabney ran past first base and was on his way to second when the left fielder picked up the ball. He threw it to Benny, but it was way over Benny's head.

Benny chased after the ball and Dabney ran to third base. Benny threw the ball to the third baseman, who dropped it. And Dabney ran home.

Dabney jumped and yelled, "I did it! I did it! I hit a home run."

After Dabney ran home, Benny kept shaking his head and punching his glove. He wasn't happy.

That was the last run we scored. Our half of the inning was over. We were winning two to nothing. The Birds had only three outs to go.

I ran back to my position in right field. I think our pitcher was getting tired. The first

Birds batter hit the ball hard and deep into center field. We were lucky. Our center fielder was standing right there and caught it.

There was one out.

The next batter hit the ball to our left fielder. He caught it.

There were two outs.

But the next batter got a hit. And the next two batters were walked. The bases were loaded with Birds when the next batter walked to the plate. It was Benny.

This seemed just like a game in his Benny, Benny League. A hit by Benny could win the game.

Benny took a few practice swings. Then he waited for the first pitch. It was low. Ball one.

I knew Benny would just love to get a hit. And even though I was on the other team, I was rooting for him. I imagined Benny hitting a home run. He would be clapping and saying again and again, "That Baker is great."

Benny swung at the second pitch. He missed. That was the first strike.

I imagined Benny announcing, "This is it. It's all up to Benny Baker. He steps up to the plate. He waits for the pitch. He swings. He hits the ball hard."

Benny *did* swing at the next pitch. He *did* hit it hard. The ball flew high over the first baseman's head. It was coming in my direction. I ran back for it. The ball was going over my

head, too. I reached up with my glove and jumped as high as I could. Then I fell to the ground.

Benny kept running.

One of the other players on our team came over to me. He reached into my glove and took out the ball. I had caught it!

First I was excited. We had won the game. But then I thought about Benny. I knew that he really wanted to hit a home run.

The other players on my team ran to me. Before I knew what was happening, I was being carried on someone's shoulders. All the Gum Drops, Mr. Cotton, and some people from the stands crowded around me and cheered.

I felt like a fish swimming in the ocean. I was surrounded by other fish and we were all swimming in the same direction.

"Swim that way," I told the person carrying me. I pointed toward the stands.

"Swim?"

"She means 'go'," someone said. "Jane is real interested in underwater things. At school we call her 'Jane, Jane, Fish Nut'."

I saw my parents coming out of the stands. They were cheering for me, too.

Then I saw Benny. He and his friends were sitting on their team bench near first base. They weren't cheering.

"Swim the other way. Swim the other way," I told the person carrying me. But she didn't listen.

I was worried what Benny would say when I came near him. I knew he wanted to get a hit real bad. But, because of me, he was out and his team lost the game.

Benny looked up and saw me. Then he pointed to me and told his friends, "*That* Baker is great."

I smiled. So did Benny.

Later, when we were going home in the car, Benny told Mom and Dad, "Jane made a real great catch. I wish she were on our team."

"I've seen you make some great catches, too," Dad told Benny.

"What will you do this afternoon?" Mom asked.

"There's a tv program I want to watch. It's about plankton," I said. "They're tiny animals and plants that float around in the ocean."

"I want to watch a baseball game," Benny said.

"Baseball!" Mom said. "You played baseball all morning. Can't you think about anything else?"

Dad and I shook our heads and said, "No." Then Dad and I said, "That's why they call him 'Benny, Benny, Baseball Nut'."